BOOM!

By **Mary Lyn Ray**

Pictures by **Steven Salerno**

Disney · Hyperion Books
New York

Printed in Malaysia

First Edition
H106-9333-5-13074
1 3 5 7 9 10 8 6 4 2

Library of Congress Cataloging-in-Publication Data

Ray, Mary Lyn.
  Boom! : big, big thunder & one small dog / by Mary Lyn Ray ; illustrated by Steven Salerno. — 1st ed.
     p. cm.
  Summary: Rosie, a little dog, is afraid of nothing except thunder and during one very bad storm, she
discovers that the boy who she lives with is frightened, too.
  ISBN 978-1-4231-6238-4
[1. Thunder—Fiction. 2. Dogs—Fiction. 3. Courage—Fiction.] I. Salerno, Steven, ill. II. Title.
  PZ7.R210154Boo 2013
  [E]—dc23   2012030914

Reinforced binding

Visit www.disneyhyperionbooks.com

For every dog who would hide from thunder
—M.L.R.

To the family dog, Jasper
—S.S.

Although Rosie was a small dog,
she was usually very brave—
just like the boy she knew best.

She wasn't afraid of tigers, though she didn't have to prove this because no tigers lived nearby.

She wasn't afraid of orange cats.
Or orangutans—at least, not their pictures in books.

She wasn't afraid of garbage collectors,
postmen or postwomen,
policemen or policewomen,
firemen or firewomen,
or even the siren on
fire trucks.

A car wash or waves or taking a bath:
she wasn't afraid of those.

She had no fear of shadows at night.

RRrrrRRRRRrr

Rrrr

Feather duster? Vacuum cleaner?
She wasn't afraid of those.

But she *was* afraid of thunder.

When a storm began to rumble, this small dog
who was usually a brave dog wasn't.

The boy offered her a biscuit.
But Rosie wouldn't eat it.

There was no comfort in a biscuit.

The boy tried singing songs.

But there was no comfort in a song.

The boy told her thunder was watermelons rolling from a watermelon truck.

He told her it was a block fort falling.

He told her it was hot clouds popping
like popcorn.

But the little dog knew.
It was the big, big sky growling big, big growls.

She crept under a table.

Except it wasn't safe there. The sky could still see her.

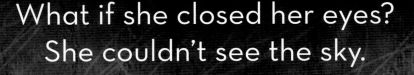

What if she closed her eyes?
She couldn't see the sky.

BOOM!

But the sky could see her.

The boy may have felt a little frightened, too.

The thunder was big thunder.

He thought about a safe place.
And then he knew just where to go. His room.
A little square room with his bold blue bed in the center.

There he lay against the dog and the dog lay against him, and they made a circle they filled exactly—

where they waited for the thunder to tire.

But the thunder wasn't tired.

IT CLAPPED, GROWLED,

IT CLAPPED, GROWLED,

AND CRACKED...

until it **CLAPPED** one last, dismissive clap.

It **GROWLED** one small, last growl.

And it **YAWNED**.

The boy heard the calm. He heard the quiet.
So he told the little dog, who heard it, too.

And Rosie barked at the stillness.

A brave dog again.